# Jane Eyre

CHARLOTTE BRONTË

SADDLEBACK
PUBLISHING · INC.

# Saddleback's *Illustrated Classics*™

Three Watson
Irvine, CA 92618-2767
Website: www.sdlback.com

*ISBN 1-56254-912-X*

Printed in China.

# Welcome to
# Saddleback's *Illustrated Classics*™

We are proud to welcome you to Saddleback's *Illustrated Classics*™. Saddleback's *Illustrated Classics*™ was designed specifically for the classroom to introduce readers to many of the great classics in literature. Each text, written and adapted by teachers and researchers, has been edited using the Dale-Chall vocabulary system. In addition, much time and effort has been spent to ensure that these high-interest stories retain all of the excitement, intrigue, and adventure of the original books.

With these graphically *Illustrated Classics*™, you learn what happens in the story in a number of different ways. One way is by reading the words a character says. Another way is by looking at the drawings of the character. The artist can tell you what kind of person a character is and what he or she is thinking or feeling.

This series will help you to develop confidence and a sense of accomplishment as you finish each novel. The stories in Saddleback's *Illustrated Classics*™ are fun to read. And remember, fun motivates!

# Overview

Everyone deserves to read the best literature our language has to offer. Saddleback's *Illustrated Classics*™ was designed to acquaint readers with the most famous stories from the world's greatest authors, while teaching essential skills. You will learn how to:

- Establish a purpose for reading
- Use prior knowledge
- Evaluate your reading
- Listen to the language as it is written
- Extend literary and language appreciation through discussion and writing activities

Reading is one of the most important skills you will ever learn. It provides the key to all kinds of information. By reading the *Illustrated Classics*™ , you will develop confidence and the self-satisfaction that comes from accomplishment— a solid foundation for any reader.

# Step-By-Step

The following is a simple guide to using and enjoying each of your *Illustrated Classics*™. To maximize your use of the learning activities provided, we suggest that you follow these steps:

1. *Listen!* We suggest that you listen to the read-along. (At this time, please ignore the beeps.) You will enjoy this wonderfully dramatized presentation.

2. *Pre-reading Activities.* After listening to the audio presentation, the pre-reading activities in the Activity Book prepare you for reading the story by setting the scene, introducing more difficult vocabulary words, and providing some short exercises.

3. *Reading Activities.* Now turn to the "While you are reading" portion of the Activity Book, which directs you to make a list of story-related facts. Read-along while listening to the audio presentation. (This time pay attention to the beeps, as they indicate when each page should be turned.)

4. *Post-reading Activities.* You have successfully read the story and listened to the audio presentation. Now answer the multiple-choice questions and other activities in the Activity Book.

**Remember,**

*"Today's readers are tomorrow's leaders"*

# about the author

Charlotte Brontë was born in Yorkshire, England, in 1816. Her father was a minister, and her mother was a frail woman who died when Charlotte was five.

Charlotte and three of her sisters were sent to a school nearby where conditions were so bad that two of them grew sick and died. Many believe that Charlotte used this school as a model for Lowood in *Jane Eyre.*

When her education was complete, Charlotte and her sister Emily planned to open a school for girls. But no one applied to the school, and the sisters were forced to give it up. Then a new idea occurred to them. Charlotte had been writing stories since she was a child; finally she decided to publish one. In 1847, under the pen name of Currer Bell, Charlotte's novel *Jane Eyre* was printed. It was an instant success.

Her financial worries were over, but Charlotte had other sufferings to endure. Her brother and her two sisters died within a short time, leaving her alone. Yet she managed to write two more novels, *Shirley* and *Villette.* Then in 1854 she married Arthur Bell Nicholls, her father's assistant minister.

Charlotte's happiness as an author and a wife, however, was cut short. After only a year of marriage, she died in 1855 at the age of thirty-nine.

# Saddleback's *Illustrated Classics*™

Charlotte Brontë

# Jane Eyre

Bessie

Mr. Rochester

Jane Eyre

Mrs. Fairfax

St. John Rivers

This is my story. As a child I was left an orphan in the care of my mother's brother. All was well until he died. He left a widow and three children who had room in their house, but not in their hearts, for me.

It was a rainy winter day at Gateshead Hall. My cousins Eliza, John, and Georgiana gathered around their mother in the drawing room.

See, Mama? He can sit up!

Yes, dear.

I was not allowed to join them.

No, Jane. . .not until you can do what you're told!

What does Bessie say I have done?

You see! Always questioning your elders! Be seated some-where, and remain silent until you can speak nicely.

With a book, I settled on a windowseat in the next room. I was happy.

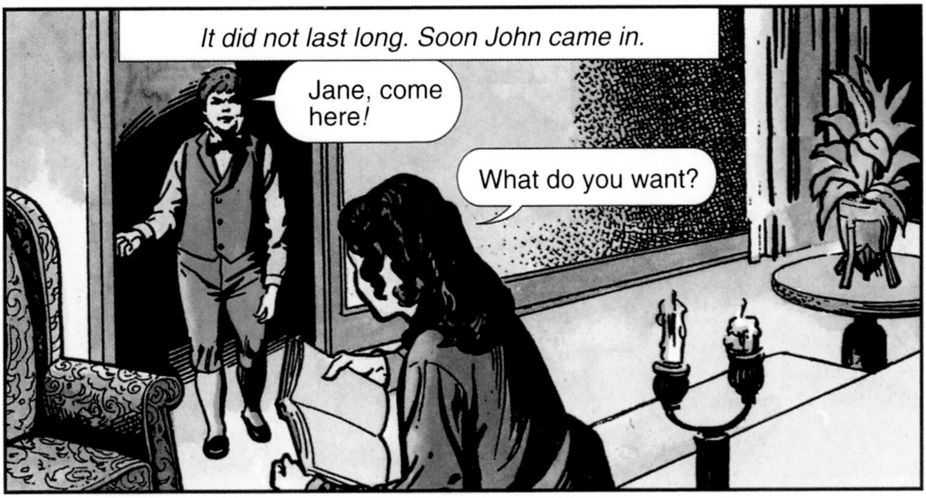
It did not last long. Soon John came in.
Jane, come here!
What do you want?

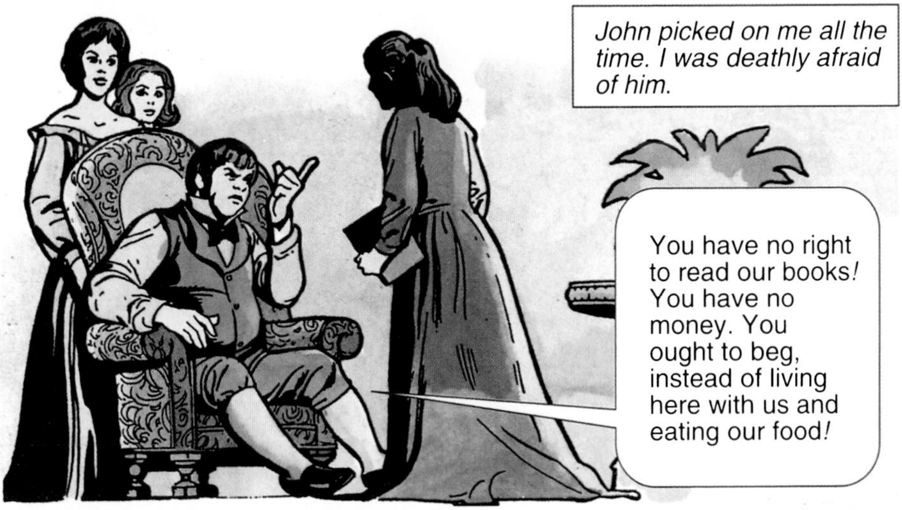
John picked on me all the time. I was deathly afraid of him.
You have no right to read our books! You have no money. You ought to beg, instead of living here with us and eating our food!

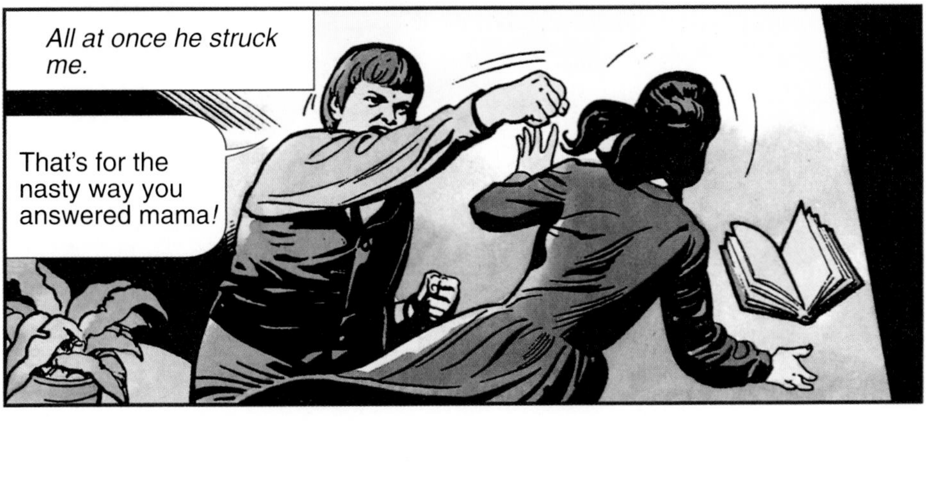
All at once he struck me.
That's for the nasty way you answered mama!

Then, picking up the book, John threw it at me.

And that is for reading my books!

For once, I answered back. I had been reading a history of Rome.

John rushed at me.

What? Did you hear what she said, Eliza and Georgiana? Wait till I get over there!

Wicked boy! You are like the Roman emperors!

He grasped me by the hair. Angrily I fought back.

Mrs. Reed arrived, followed by her maid Abbot, and Bessie the nurse. We were quickly separated.

What a fury, to fly at Master John!

Did anybody ever see such a thing?

Take her away to the red room, and lock her in!

I was carried upstairs, struggling all the way.

She never did so before.

It was always in her! She's an under-handed little thing!

12

*In the red room, nine years before, Mr. Reed had died and had lain in state. It was an elegant, cold room, and was seldom used.*

You must know, Miss, you owe a great deal to Mrs. Reed. If she turned you out, you would go to the poor-house!

Just because she allows you to be brought up with the Misses and Master John, it doesn't make you their equal. They will have a lot of money, and you will have none!

It is your place to be humble!

It's for your own good!

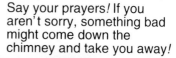

Say your prayers! If you aren't sorry, something bad might come down the chimney and take you away!

*They left, locking the door. My head ached and bled. I sat trying to think.*

Eliza and Georgiana are selfish and spoiled; John is cruel to me and to everyone! But they are loved and praised and never punished!

I try to be good, but I am always punished. It's just not right!

*Mr. Reed had been my uncle, my mother's brother. When my parents died soon after my birth, he took me into his own home. And at his death, he had made Mrs. Reed promise to bring me up as one of her own children.*

*I walked to the window.*

If Mr. Reed were here, he would treat me kindly! But he is out there in a grave in the churchyard.

He died in that very bed. If he were here he would be a ghost! No! No! I don't want to see him!

A beam of light slanted into the room, glided to the ceiling, and came to rest over my head. I was terrified.

Help! Help!

Then I heard footsteps and the key turned.

Are you hurt? Did you see something?

What dreadful noise!

Take me out! Let me go to my room!

Oh, I saw a light, and I thought a ghost would come!

Then Mrs. Reed appeared.

What is all this?

I gave orders that Jane Eyre should be left in the red room until I came for her!

Miss Jane screamed so loud, ma'am!

Oh, Aunt, have pity! Punish me some other way!

Silence! This outburst is hateful!

I heard the door lock and the footsteps move away.

I fell to the floor in a faint.

The next thing I remembered was a red light and the sound of voices.

Where am I?

In your own bed. You are all right now.

16

Well, who am I?

Mr. Lloyd, sir – the apothecary.

She'll do very well now, See that she is not upset tonight. I will call again tomorrow.

*Talking to me the next day, Mr. Lloyd learned that I was very unhappy and would like to go to school. He told this to Mrs. Reed. Several weeks later I was brought to her in the drawing room.*

This is the little girl I told you about, Mr. Brocklehurst.

There is no sight so sad as that of a naughty child!

I wish her to be brought up very simply. She must be made useful, be kept humble.

I take care to do this at Lowood! Plain fare, simple dress, hardy and active habits. . .

So it was that I was sent to Lowood, a charity-school for orphans. Bessie put me on the public coach early one morning.

Goodbye, Bessie...you've been kind to me.

Goodbye, Miss Jane! I'm fonder of you than of all the others!

After travelling all day, I was tired when I arrived. I noticed little more than the long dormitory where we slept two in a bed.

You will sleep here with me tonight.

A loud bell awakened us before daylight. It was very cold.

Dress yourself, then get in line to wash your face.

18

Then we went to the class-room for an hour's work. At last, about daybreak, another bell sent us to the dining room.

Smell it! The porridge is burnt again!

I had eaten little the day before. I was hungry.

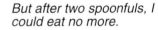
But after two spoonfuls, I could eat no more.

It's terrible!

Like rotten potatoes!

The eighty girls were divided into four classes, all meeting in the same room.

You will sit here, Jane, in the lowest class.

*At noon Miss Temple, the principal, rose and spoke to us.*

You had a breakfast this morning you could not eat; you must be hungry.

I have ordered that a lunch of bread and cheese be served to all.

*After this welcome lunch, we went to the garden for some exercise. Here I made a friend, Helen Burns.*

Will you tell me something about the school?

Anything I can.

"Lowood School. Rebuilt by Naomi Brocklehurst of Brocklehurst Hall." What does that mean?

She was Mr. Brocklehurst's mother. He runs everything here.

Then the school does not belong to Miss Temple?

Oh, no! She must answer to Mr. Brocklehurst for everything.

Why do all the girls look so much alike?

We make our own clothes – all from the same materials and the same patterns.

*One afternoon Mr. Brocklehurst visited the school.*

I find in settling the accounts that a lunch of bread and cheese has been served to the girls. How is this?

I ordered it, sir. Breakfast was so badly prepared that they could not eat it.

Madam, my plan is to make these girls hardy, patient, and humble! A little thing like burnt porridge should be allowed every now and then!

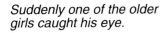

*Suddenly one of the older girls caught his eye.*

What is this? Red hair, ma'am, curled – curled all over!

That is Julia Severn. Her hair curls naturally.

I wish the hair to be arranged plainly! That girl's hair must be cut short enough never to curl again!

Mr. Brocklehurst was a dreadful man. I was very afraid of him. But I worked hard, learned my lessons, and was promoted to a higher class. I began to learn French and drawing. I made many friends. At last I began to be happy.

*Spring came. It was warm, and the world blossomed.*

Oh, Helen it's lovely! It's warm!

*But the warm weather brought illness. Typhus turned the school into a hospital.*

More than half the pupils are ill!

The building is in an unhealthy place. The girls are not fed enough. Their bodies cannot fight off the disease.

*Before the sickness had run it's course, there were many deaths, among them Helen Burns. But some good came out of all our suffering.*

All of us were shocked to learn about life at Lowood.

Many people in the county have raised the money for a new school. It will be built in a much better place.

Everything is to be improved. Mr. Brocklehurst will no longer have so much power*!*

I am so thankful*!* Lowood can become a truly noble school*!*

*And so it proved to be. I re-mained there for six years as a pupil, receiving a fine education. I stayed on for two more years as a teacher. And Miss Temple's friendship was always my greatest joy.*

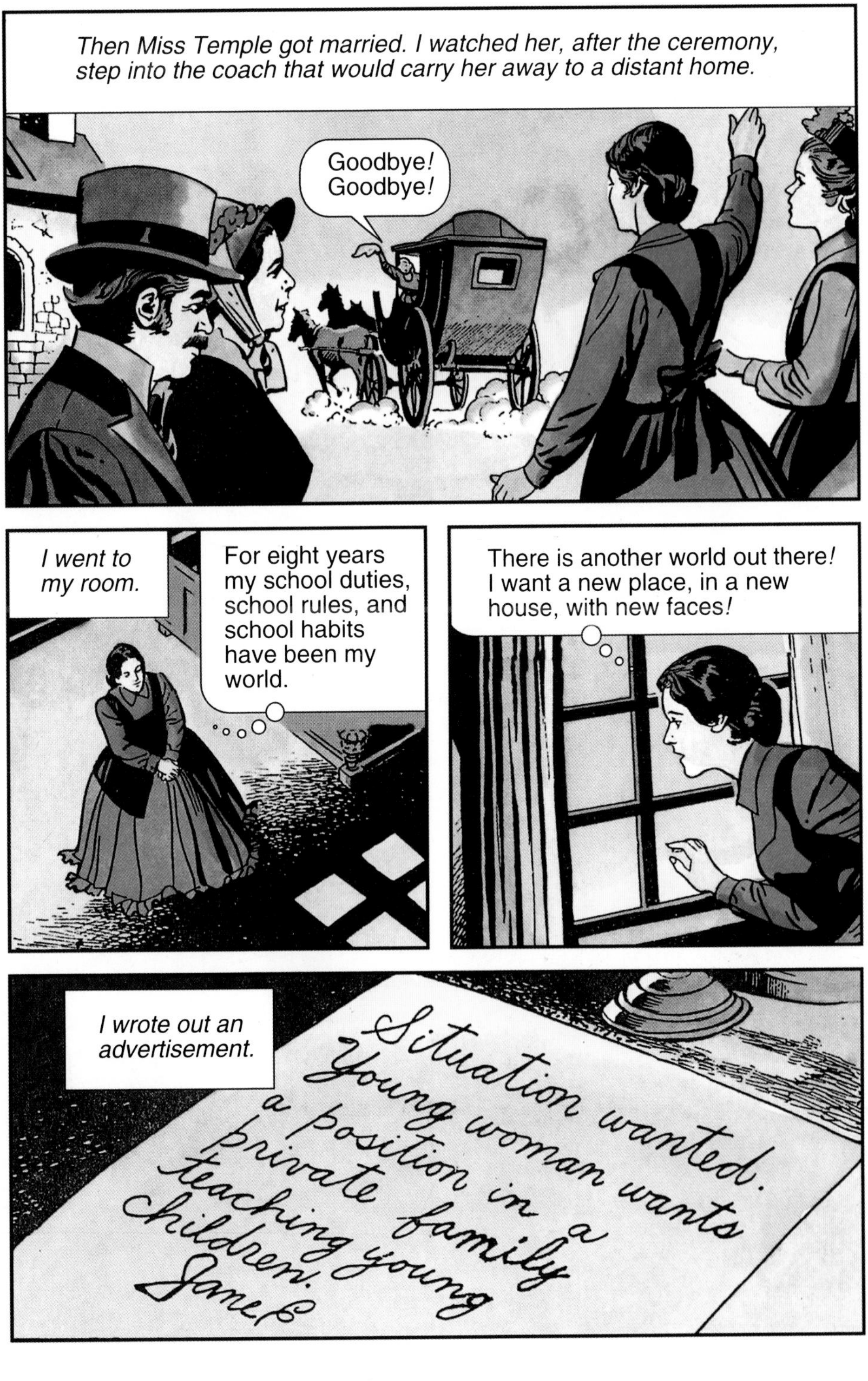
Then Miss Temple got married. I watched her, after the ceremony, step into the coach that would carry her away to a distant home.
Goodbye! Goodbye!
I went to my room.
For eight years my school duties, school rules, and school habits have been my world.
There is another world out there! I want a new place, in a new house, with new faces!
I wrote out an advertisement.
Situation wanted.
Young woman wants
a position in a
private family
teaching young
children.
Jane E.

*I mailed it to the newspaper. A week later I visited the Lowton Post Office.*

Are there any letters for J. E.?

There is just one.

*It was not until bedtime that I could read my letter.*

One pupil, a little girl... thirty pounds a year... references... Mrs. Fairfax of Thornfield!

*I told the principal of my chance at a new job. She spoke to Mr. Brocklehurst, who said that Mrs. Reed, as my guardian, must agree.*

Mrs. Reed writes that you may do as you wish. She long ago gave up any interest in your life.

I've neither seen nor heard from any of the Reeds since I came to Lowood. I was sure they would not care.

*Soon I prepared to leave Lowood. My last evening arrived.*

Miss, a person downstairs wishes to see you.

*I went to the teachers' sitting-room. A woman took my hand.*

I would have known you anywhere! And you've not quite forgotten me, I think, Miss Jane?

*In another second I was kissing her.*

Bessie! Bessie! Bessie!

*Bessie told me her own news, and that of the Reeds.*

Did Mrs. Reed send you, Bessie?

Oh, no! I've often wanted to see you. Then when I heard you were moving far away, I thought I would come and say goodbye.

I am afraid you do not like what I have become, Bessie!

No, Miss Jane. You are quite a lady, and ever so smart! You'll do well, even without your rich relatives!

Have you ever heard anything from your father's family, the Eyres?

Never in my life.

Missus always said they were poor and low-class. But seven years ago, a Mr. Eyre came to Gateshead and wanted to see you. He was as much of a gentleman as any of the Reeds could ever be!

He was sorry to hear that you were away at school. He was leaving in a day or two for another country.

What country?

An island far away. . . where they make wine. . . Madeira, that's it!

Well, I have never heard from him.

*We talked of old times for an hour or more. Then Bessie left for home, and I went to bed. The next morning I mounted the coach which would take me to new duties and a new life.*

After a sixteen-hour drive I reached my goal, a country house outside of Millcote.

So this is Thornfield Hall!

The maid showed me to a cozy sitting-room.

Come in, my dear! You must be cold.

Mrs. Fairfax, I suppose?

Yes. Do sit down! I will order you a hot drink and something to eat!

I had expected to see someone very formal, but she treated me like a visitor. Mrs. Fairfax paid more attention to my comfort than I had ever before received!

*After my late supper she led me upstairs through great, dark hallways to my bedroom.*

This is the room next to mine. It is only a small apartment, but I thought you would prefer it to one of the front rooms, grand as they are!

Thank you! That was very kind.

*The next morning I arose early. I found my way downstairs and stepped out through an open door to look at my new home.*

A gentleman's manor house! It is not a nobleman's home, but it is quite lovely anyway!

*It was here that Mrs. Fairfax found me.*

You are an early riser! How do you like Thornfield?

Very Much!

Yes, a pretty place. But I fear it will run down, unless Mr. Rochester should decide to live here the year round.

Mr. Rochester? Who is he?

The owner of Thornfield! Did you not know?

I thought Thornfield belonged to you!

Bless you, child! I am only the housekeeper... although a distant relative of his.

And the little girl, my pupil?

She is Adele Varens, a French child, Mr. Rochester's ward. Here she comes now, with her nurse.

Come, Adele, speak to the lady who is to teach you.

C'est ma gouvernante!

After breakfast, Adele and I went to the library, which would serve as our schoolroom.

Books, a piano, an easel, globes we shall do very well here.

I am so happy that you speak my language well, mademoiselle!

Later Mrs. Fairfax showed me through the house.

What a beautiful room!

I have opened a window to air it.

Things grow damp in rooms that are seldom used.

You keep things in wonderful order! One would think the rooms were open every day.

Though Mr. Rochester's visits are rare, they are always unexpected. I like things to be ready when he comes.

*I followed her through many grand chambers, then through the attics and onto the roof for a fine view. Returning, I awaited her in an attic hall.*

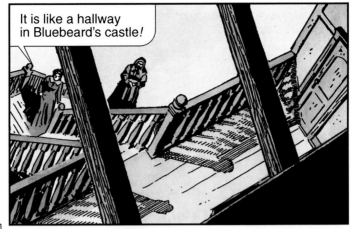

It is like a hallway in Bluebeard's castle*!*

*Then I heard a sound. . . a loud, strange laugh.*

Ha-ha-HA-HA*!*

Mrs. Fairfax*!* Did you hear it? Does Thornfield Hall have a ghost?

No ghosts at Thornfield, my dear. It is likely one of the servants. . .perhaps Grace Poole.

Too much noise, Grace. Remember your orders.

Yes ma'am.

She is a servant who sews and helps with the housemaid's work.

She is not very ghost-like*!*

*October, November, December passed. Mrs. Fairfax, Adele, and I got along well. One January afternoon I set out for a walk.*

I am happy, and yet I wonder what lies in the towns beyond the hills.

*As I started to walk again, a horseman appeared.*

*Suddenly, with a clatter, the horse slipped on some ice.*

What the deuce...

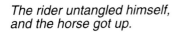

*The rider untangled himself, and the horse got up.*

Are you hurt, sir?

Down, Pilot!

If you are hurt and want help, I can fetch someone from Thornfield Hall.

Thank you, I shall manage. No broken bones, only a sprain.

I cannot leave you alone until I see you are able to ride.

Very well, then... help me to my horse.

You should be at home yourself. Go quickly!

Back at Thornfield Hall, I went to Mrs. Fairfax's room. She was not there, but a great dog lay in front of the fireplace.

He came to me, wagging his tail. I rang for the maid.

What dog is this?

He came with the master, Mr. Rochester. He has just arrived!

Master's horse slipped on the ice and his ankle is sprained. The doctor is coming.

I did not see Mr. Rochester that night or the next day, but the silence of the Hall was broken by knocks at the door, bells, footsteps, voices. Adele was not easy to teach that day.

Sit down, Adele! He is busy.

*Later, Mrs. Fairfax came in.*

Mr. Rochester would be glad if you and your pupil would take tea with him this evening.

Should I change my dress?

Yes. I always dress for the evening when he is here.

*Mrs. Fairfax went with me to the drawing room.*

Here is Miss Eyre, sir.

Let Miss Eyre be seated.

*Soon the tea tray was brought in. Mrs. Fairfax asked me to hand Mr. Rochester his cup.*

Monsieur Rochester, did you bring a gift for Mademoiselle Eyre?

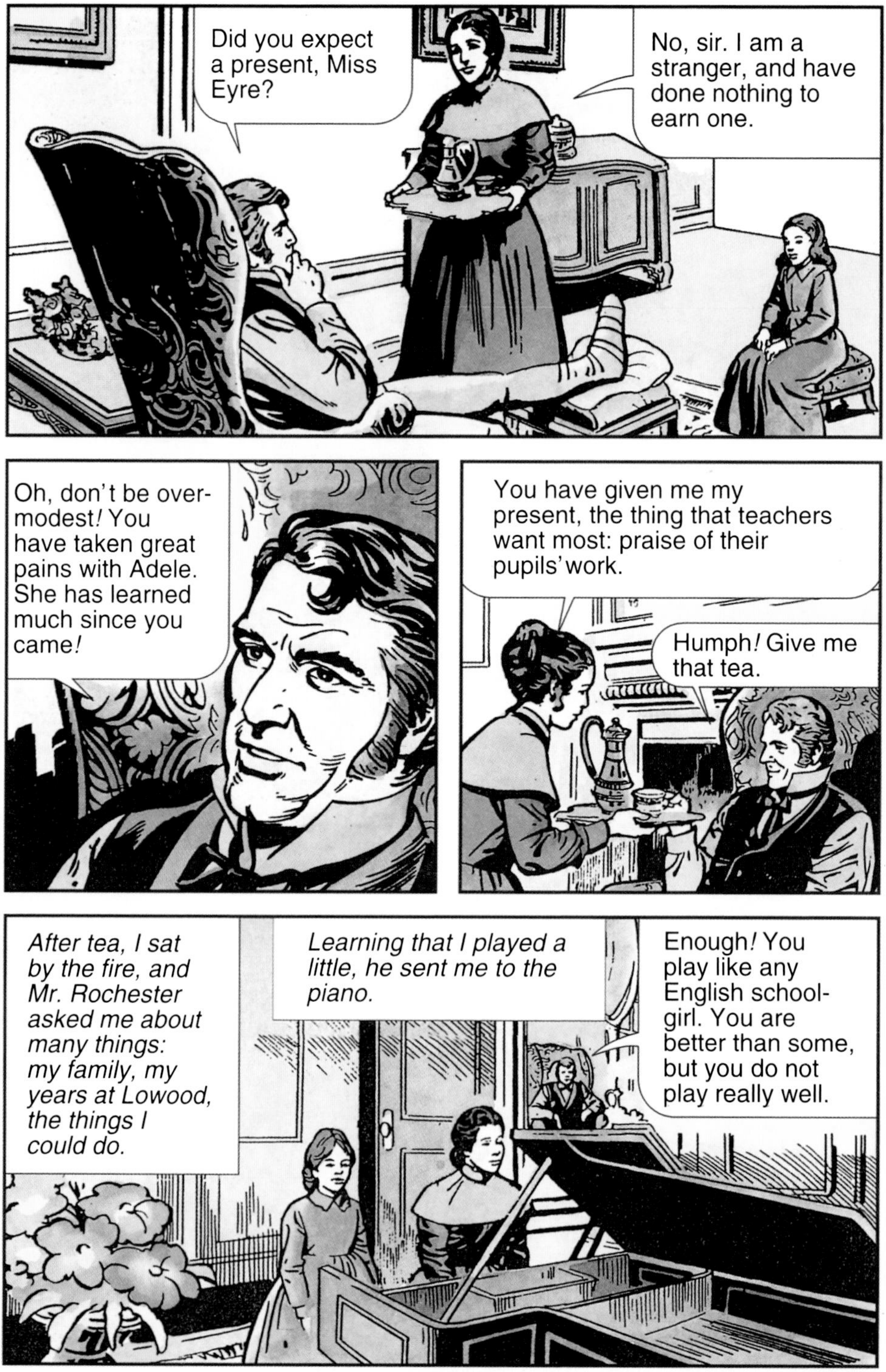
Did you expect a present, Miss Eyre?
No, sir. I am a stranger, and have done nothing to earn one.
Oh, don't be over-modest! You have taken great pains with Adele. She has learned much since you came!
You have given me my present, the thing that teachers want most: praise of their pupils' work.
Humph! Give me that tea.
*After tea, I sat by the fire, and Mr. Rochester asked me about many things: my family, my years at Lowood, the things I could do.*
*Learning that I played a little, he sent me to the piano.*
Enough! You play like any English school-girl. You are better than some, but you do not play really well.

Adele showed me some sketches she said were yours. Did a teacher help you?

No indeed!

Ah, that pricks your pride! Well, let me see the others you have done!

*Mr. Rochester studied each sketch and painting carefully He set aside three.*

Were you happy when you painted these pictures?

To paint them was to have one of the greatest joys I have ever known!

But I was upset by the contrast between my ideas and my work.

You have captured the shadow of your thought, and the thoughts are elfish! Those eyes must have come from a dream... And who taught you to paint wind?

*Then, sweeping the drawings into their folder, Mr. Rochester looked at his watch.*

It is nine o'clock! Why are you letting Adele sit up for so long? Take her to bed.

*Later I joined Mrs. Fairfax in her room.*

What did you think of Mr. Rochester?

He is very changeable, is he not?

Yes, but he had had troubles. As he grew up, his father and elder brother were unfair to him.

He broke with them and traveled for many years. Then, nine years ago, when his brother died, he inherited Thornfield Hall.

He also told me something of his past life.

In the days that passed, I had other talks with Mr. Rochester. He liked to talk about the world and its beauties to people who had seen only a small part of it.

In the course of your life, Jane, you must have had many friends tell you their secrets.

How can you guess all this, sir?

I know it. You listen with great understanding. I talk to you as freely as if I were writing in my diary.

I am fighting within myself. Life dares me to like Thornfield – dares me to stay here!

*That night I could not sleep. I kept thinking of his look when he spoke of staying at Thornfield.*

Will he leave again soon? Mrs. Fairfax said he seldom stays longer than two weeks. He has been here eight weeks already...

If he goes. . . if he is absent. . . how sad the fine days of spring, summer, and fall will seem*!*

*I put out my candle and lay down. I heard the clock strike two. Then there was a devilish laugh.*

Ha-ha-HA-HA HA*!*

Was that Grace Poole? Is she insane?

I am frightened*!* I will dress and go to Mrs. Fairfax*!*

*When I opened my door I saw no one... only a candle burning on the hall floor.*

Smoke! And I smell something burning!

*Forgetting everything else, I hurried to Mr. Rochester's room.*

Wake up! Wake up!

*The smoke had made him groggy. I rushed for his basin and pitcher and emptied them onto the bed.*

*Thank God, I could put out the fire.*

What the devil! Is there a flood?

No, sir, but there has been a fire. Get up. I will light a candle.

*As Mr. Rochester looked at the damage, I told him what had happened.*

Shall I call Mrs. Fairfax? Or the servants?

No! Wrap up in my cloak, sit there, and be still. I must pay a visit to the third floor.

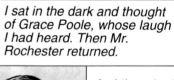

*I sat in the dark and thought of Grace Poole, whose laugh I had heard. Then Mr. Rochester returned.*

As I thought, it is Grace Poole, a strange woman. Say nothing about this to anyone. I must think.

You have saved my life! And I am pleased to owe you that!

You owe me nothing, sir.

I knew you would do me good; I saw it in your eyes when I first looked at you. My dear protector, good night!

Good night, sir!

*But the day passed as usual. I met Mrs. Fairfax in her room for tea.*

*There was a strange sound in his voice, strange fire in his look. I went to bed but not to sleep. On the next day I both wished and feared to see him again.*

Well, Mr. Rochester has had a good day for his journey.

Journey! I did not know he had gone anywhere.

Yes, to Mr. Eshton's place. There is quite a party. I should think he might stay a week or more.

Are there ladies there?

Oh, yes. And one of them is Miss Blanche Ingram. She is a most beautiful woman, and is admired also for her great talents.

44

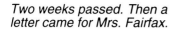
*Two weeks passed. Then a letter came for Mrs. Fairfax.*

Well – sometimes we are too quiet, but we'll be busy enough now!

Mr. Rochester is returning?

In three days – and bringing with him most of the fine people from the Eshton party.
All the best bedrooms are to be prepared. . . everything cleaned. . . extra kitchen help hired. . .

*On the stated afternoon, the party arrived.*

*Soon the house was full of happy voices. In the hallways the maids and valets of the visitors rushed about. Mrs. Fairfax brought me a message.*

Mr. Rochester asks that you bring Adele to the drawing room after dinner each evening.

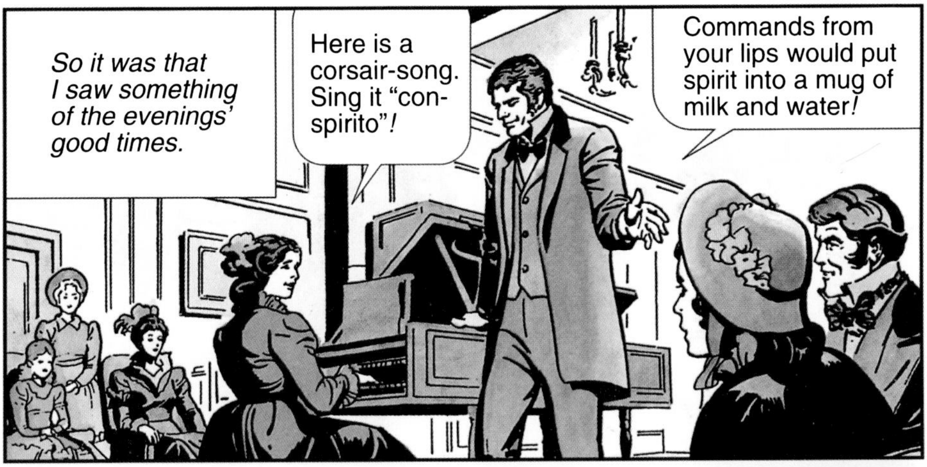
So it was that I saw something of the evenings' good times.
Here is a corsair-song. Sing it "con-spirito"!
Commands from your lips would put spirit into a mug of milk and water!

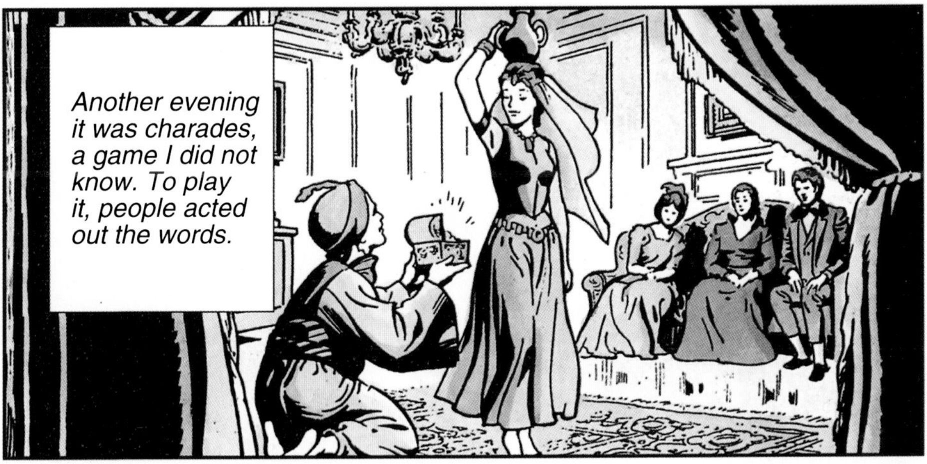
Another evening it was charades, a game I did not know. To play it, people acted out the words.

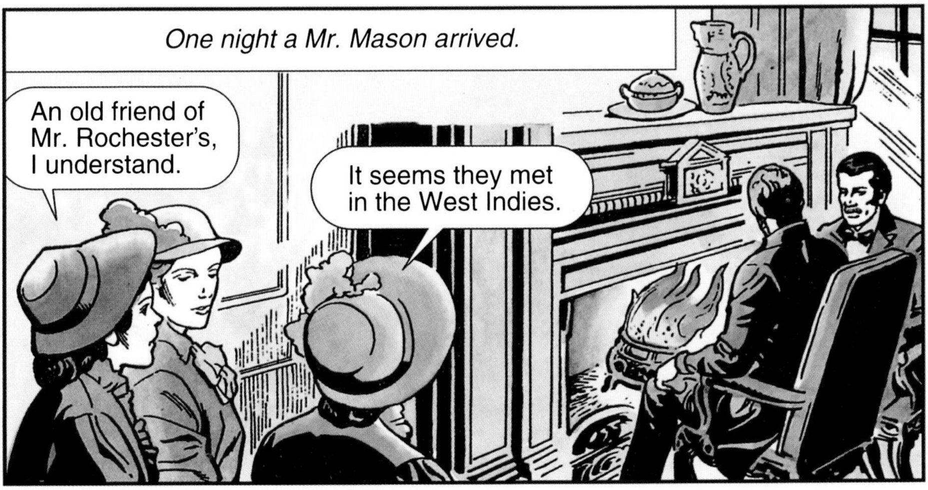
One night a Mr. Mason arrived.
An old friend of Mr. Rochester's, I understand.
It seems they met in the West Indies.

That night I was awakened by a terrible cry.

Help! Help! Help!

Rochester! For God's sake, come!

It is from the third floor!

In a moment the hallway was full of excited people.

Who is it? Who is hurt? Is it a fire?

It's all right! Calm down!

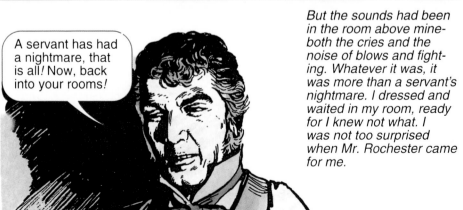

A servant has had a nightmare, that is all! Now, back into your rooms!

But the sounds had been in the room above mine—both the cries and the noise of blows and fighting. Whatever it was, it was more than a servant's nightmare. I dressed and waited in my room, ready for I knew not what. I was not too surprised when Mr. Rochester came for me.

*In a third floor room an inner door, usually covered by a curtain, stood open.*

It sounds like an animal growling in there!

Never mind! I will lock the door.

*He led me around a large bed.*

Mr. Mason!

He will be all right. But you must stay with him while I ride for the doctor.

*It seemed forever that I sat beside Mason, wiping away the blood and holding smelling salts to his nose when he felt faint. But at last dawn came, and Mr. Rochester and the doctor arrived.*

He will be all right – it is mostly loss of blood. But there have been teeth here, as well as a knife!

She bit me – like a tiger!

I warned you to be on your guard!

*Mr. Rochester wanted Mason to be away before everyone woke up. We helped him down to a waiting carriage after the doctor had finished.*

Goodbye, Rochester. Let her be treated as tenderly as may be...

I do my best. I have done it, and will do it.

48

Only a short time later I received a message from Bessie at Gateshead. My cousin John Reed, having gambled away most of the family's fortune, had shot himself. The shock had given his mother a stroke, and she kept calling for Jane Eyre.

I went at once to find Mr. Rochester.

I suppose I must give you leave to go. But promise you will return in a week!

I promise to return, sir. But perhaps not in a week's time.

Indeed, when I arrived at Gateshead my aunt was very ill. It was more than two weeks before she could tell me what she wanted.

Go to my dressing-case. Open it, take out the letter you will see, and read it.

I obeyed her orders and read the following, dated three years back:

Madam:
I wish to adopt my niece, Jane Eyre. I want to bring her here to Madeira to live. I wish to leave my fortune to her.
John Eyre

I could not bear to make you wealthy! I wrote him that Jane Eyre had died of typhus fever at Lowood. Now act as you please. . .

Love me or hate me as you will, Aunt. You have my full forgiveness.

Mrs. Reed died that night. I had hoped to leave after the funeral, but stayed on to give my cousins what help I could. A month had passed before I reached Thornfield again.

It was a beautiful summer evening as I left the coach and walked across the fields. My heart beat faster as I saw a familiar figure.

Jane! Is it you or a dream?

It is I, sir.

Jane, never leave me again! Will you marry me?

Are you serious? Do you truly love me?

I do; if only an oath will satisfy you, I swear it!

Then, sir, I will marry you.

The next few days passed in a happy dream as Mr. Rochester made his plans.

We shall be married in four weeks. The wedding will take place quietly in the village church below.

I feel so surprised I hardly know what to say!

Will Mademoiselle wear satin and jewels?

I have sent to the bank for my family jewels. And we shall go this very day to buy Jane silks and satins!

No, no! You won't know me, sir. I will not be Jane Eyre in fancy clothes!

*Suddenly I remembered the letter from my uncle. I would write to him at once.*

I will tell my uncle that I am alive and going to be married. I would be happier if I could bring even a little money to Mr. Rochester!

*The month passed. Then, two nights before my wedding, I dreamed that Thornfield Hall was in ruins.*

*I awoke, candlelight in my eyes, to see a strange woman staring at my wedding clothes. She took my veil, and threw it over her own head.*

*She took off the veil, tore it in two, and threw it on the floor.*

*Starting for the door, she stopped at my bedside and put her candle close to my face. For the second time in my life, I fainted from terror.*

*For our wedding there were no bridesmaids, no guests. Mr. Rochester and I walked the short distance to the church, and stood before the clergyman.*

I charge you both. . .that if either knows any reason why ye may not be lawfully married, ye now say so. . .

*A voice spoke nearby.*

The marriage cannot go on. There is a good reason.

*A man came forward.*

What is it?

Simply. . . that Mr. Rochester has a wife now living!

My name is Briggs. I am a lawyer. I can prove that fifteen years ago Edward Fairfax Rochester married Bertha Mason in Spanish Town, Jamaica.

That may prove that I have been married. It does not prove that the woman is still living.

She was living three months ago.

*Another man stepped forward from the shadows.*

Mr. Mason!

I saw her at Thornfield Hall last April. I am her brother.

Enough! We can go no further. There has been gossip about the crazy woman kept at Thornfield under lock and key. She is Grace Poole's patient.

I now inform you that she is Bertha Mason, my wife. She is mad and comes from a mad family. No one told me that before I married her!

This girl knew nothing of the secret. She thought all was fair and legal.

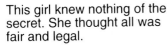

Your uncle will be glad to hear of it – if, indeed, he is still living.

My uncle! What of him? Do you know him?

Mr. Mason does. He was with your uncle when your letter arrived telling of your coming marriage. Mr. Mason revealed the facts to him.

Too ill to come to England himself, your uncle begged Mason to prevent this marriage!

We returned to Thornfield Hall. The coach, packed for our wedding trip, was unpacked, and the luggage was taken inside. I went to my room, changed from my wedding dress, and sat down to think.

What am I to do?

There was only one answer. I must leave Thornfield Hall, for my dear Edward's sake as well as my own. I must slip away unseen, for if he begged me to stay, I would not be able to leave him.

At dawn I packed a few clothes, took my purse, and crept silently out of the house.

Farewell, kind Mrs. Fairfax! Farewell, dear Adele! And God bless you, my dear master!

On the road I hailed a coach and rode for two days to Whitcross, as far as all the money in my purse would take me.

So Whitcross is only a crossroads! And I have left my things on the coach!

I was weak, tired, and hungry. I slept that night under a bush.

The next morning I ate some berries, then walked to a nearby village. I needed food and work. I entered a bake shop.

Do you know where I might find work?

No. The local factory uses only men. People who want servants have them already, and there are as many dressmakers as the town needs.

*I wandered here and there asking at other places with always the same answer. At sundown, I saw a farmer eating his supper.*

Will you give me a piece of bread? I am very hungry.

Yes. Why not?

*At dark, I was outside the village. It began to rain.*

Am I to die of want and cold?

*Suddenly, across an empty space, a light shone. Was this a sign? I tried to reach it, and found a long, low house.*

*How lucky I was! The people who lived there took me in.*

Who is it?

I found her on the doorstep.

*The Rivers family: Diana, Mary, their brother St. John, and the old servant Hannah fed me, nursed me back to health, and became my friends. St. John promised to find me work.*

I am the minister at Moreton. When I arrived, it had no school. I opened one for boys; I mean now to open one for girls. The teacher will have a two-room cottage and thirty pounds a year.

It is only a village school. The pupils will be poor girls... cottagers' children and farmers' daughters. Will you accept the job?

I accept it with all my heart*!*

*I moved into my little cottage and started the school. St. John often visited me and talked of his plans.*

Long ago I vowed to become a missionary. My father was against it, but since his death I am free to go. I shall soon leave for the East.

Come with me, Jane*!* I have watched you work here for ten months. God wanted you to be a missionary's wife*!*

I am not fit for it. God has not called me to live that way*!*

I have a woman's heart, and for you, St. John, I have only a sister's love. I cannot marry you.

Jane, you would not be sorry! I will not give up yet!

*Another day he brought a different sort of news.*

I have heard from Briggs, a London lawyer, who has news for you, Jane Eyre!

What does he want of me?

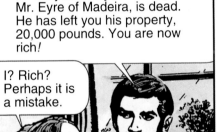

To tell you that your uncle, Mr. Eyre of Madeira, is dead. He has left you his property, 20,000 pounds. You are now rich!

I? Rich? Perhaps it is a mistake.

And why did Mr. Briggs write to you of this?

Because my mother's name was Eyre! She was your father's sister! Your Uncle John was also our Uncle John!

You, Diana, and Mary are my cousins? I have relatives at last? Oh, I am glad! I am glad!

You seem to care more about that than about the fortune!

*It was true. I was happy to have cousins whom I already loved. I arranged at once that the money should be divided among the four of us. Five thousand pounds was enough for each. Diana and Mary gave up their jobs, and we met for a happy reunion.*

In all this time I had heard no news of Mr. Rochester. Now I seemed to feel him calling me, needing me. Before I made other plans, I must know how he was.

I took a coach to Thornfield and walked across the fields toward the great house.

Eagerly I went forward. My first view would be from the front. I raised my eyes to see a lovely home – and saw a blackened ruin instead.

As in my dream, there was only a shell-like wall, paneless windows. There was no roof, no chimney. All had crashed in. And the silence of death lay around it.

I rushed to the nearby inn. The landlord would answer my questions.

Is Mr. Rochester living at Thornfield Hall now?

Oh, no, ma'am! Thornfield Hall is a ruin! It burnt down at harvest time.

There was a lady kept in the house, a lunatic. She set the fire, then died in it, despite all Mr. Rochester's efforts to rescue her.

And Mr. Rochester?

He would not leave until everyone was out, and it crashed in on him! He was taken from the ruins alive, but he is blind, and one hand is crippled.

Where is he now?

He lives at Ferndean, thirty miles away, alone with his old servants. He cut himself off from everyone!

Can you get me a carriage? I must go to Ferndean!

*At the house, I made myself known to the servants. Then I took the tray Mary had prepared, and carried it in to Mr. Rochester.*

Down, Pilot!

What is the matter?

Is that you, Mary?

Mary is in the kitchen.

Who is it? What is it? Who speaks?

Pilot knows me. Your servants know me...

His arm touched my shoulder, my neck, my waist. He took me in his arms.

Is it Jane? This is her shape, her size...

She is all here – her heart, too. God bless you, sir.

The other night sitting by my open window, I was overcome by my longing for you. I cried out loud, "Jane! Jane! Jane!"

And a voice answered – your voice – "Wait for me! I am coming!"

And I came, sir. I am here... and will never leave you!

Four days later we were married.

I now pronounce you man and wife...

*Two years later, as he dictated a letter, he came and bent over me.*

Jane, have you a shining ornament around your neck?

Yes, Edward.

And are you wearing a pale blue dress?

Yes! Edward, can you see?

*He told me that he thought one eye was improving. We went to a London doctor at once. Soon Edward recovered the sight of that eye.*

*When his first child was put into his arms, he could see that the boy had eyes like his own as they once were, large and black.*

Edward, meet your son!

*I have now been married ten years. I know what it is to live with what I love best on earth. I am greatly blessed.*

THE END